Tricksy
Pixie

D1609884

Lucy Mayflower

Hodder
Children's
Books

A division of Hachette Children's Books

Special thanks to Lucy Courtenay

Created by Hodder Children's Books and Lucy Courtenay
Text and illustrations copyright © 2007 Hodder Children's Books
Illustrations created by Artful Doodlers

First published in Great Britain in 2007
by Hodder Children's Books

1

A Catalogue record for this book is available from the British Library

ISBN – 10: 0 340 94428 5
ISBN – 13: 978 0 340 94428 8

Printed in the UK by CPI Bookmarque, Croydon, CR0 4TD

The paper and board used in this paperback by Hodder Children's Books
are natural recyclable products made from wood grown in
sustainable forests. The manufacturing processes conform to the
environmental regulations of the country of origin.

Hodder Children's Books
A division of Hachette Children's Books
338 Euston Rd, London NW1 3BH

Contents

Ambrosia Academy

WOOD STUMP

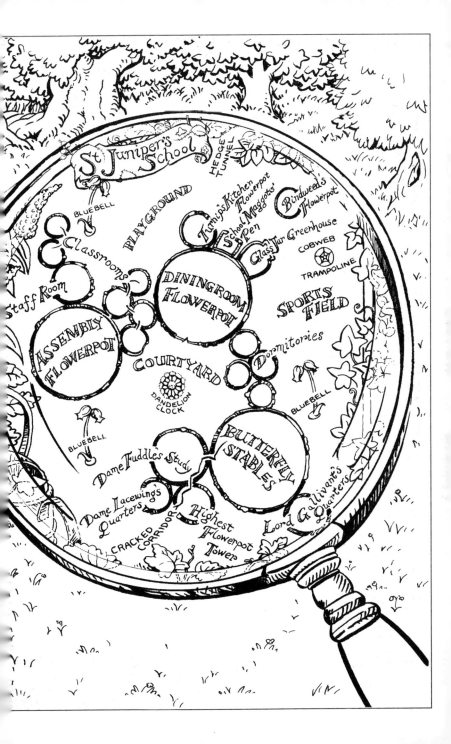

1

Snail Trail

Down at the bottom of the garden, six fairies were standing in the shadow of a flowerpot which stood all alone beside the Hedge. They were staring at a large snail in front of them. The snail was staring back.

"Good snaily," said a small fairy with a long plait down her back. She waved a leaf of grass at the snail and started backing away very slowly. "Follow the nice grass."

The snail made an interested squelchy noise and stretched out its waggling antennae.

"Wave the grass harder, Sesame," instructed a pretty black-haired fairy.

"I'm waving it as hard as I can, Brilliance," Sesame hissed.

"Shh," squeaked the smallest fairy at the back. "Bindweed will hear you!"

"No way, Tiptoe," said a scornful-looking fairy in a black and yellow dress. "Can't you hear him snoring?"

The fairies peered through a small window in the side of the flowerpot. Bindweed, janitor and gardening pixie at St Juniper's, was fast asleep on his old chair.

"He woke up when Marigold tried to tie one of the leaf-cutter ants to his ankle, Kelpie," Tiptoe said. "He was snoring then, too. Wasn't he, Nettle?"

The blonde fairy with a pair of spiders dangling from her ears nodded. "That's what Marigold said at breakfast."

"Marigold always exaggerates," said Brilliance with a shrug.

"Can't we just put a spider in his mouth?" suggested a spiky-haired fairy

2

in a bored voice. "It would be much quicker. I want to ride Pong."

Brilliance rolled her eyes. "You've got no imagination, Ping," she said. "Vetch and Onion did the mouth thing with an aphid yesterday. No – this snail plan's totally brilliant. Pelly will *have* to say that our trick was the best."

Pelly's real name was Pelargonium, but only extremely brave fairies called her that.

"Why did Pelly organise this trick challenge anyway?" Ping asked.

"Because Bindweed gave her a detention," Brilliance explained.

"I don't see why," said Kelpie. "It was a very *small* earwig."

"Still, Pelly organised it and now we've got to win it," Brilliance said with determination. "You can wait a bit longer to ride your precious dragonfly, can't you, Ping?"

"I suppose," Ping said.

"Nearly there," puffed Sesame, from the far side of the flowerpot door.

The snail lunged stickily at the grass in Sesame's hand. Its swirly shell now blocked the flowerpot doorway.

"Stop!" Brilliance commanded.

The Naughty Fairies backed a safe distance away. Brilliance cupped her hands to her mouth.

"Cooee!" Brilliance called. It was a

good impression of Dame Fuddle, head teacher of St Juniper's. "Bindweeeed, dear! The ants have got out! Come as quick as you can!"

There was a thumping, crashing noise as Bindweed fell off his chair. The Naughty Fairies heard the sound of large feet slapping across the floor of the flowerpot, and the sound of the door opening . . . and the sound of Bindweed running straight into the snail.

The fairies exploded with laughter at

the pixie's yell of rage. They sprinted
down the Sports Field, half skipping
and half flying.

"Brilliant!" Brilliance yelled, bouncing
ahead of the others. "Our Bindweed
trick was the best ever. We're so going
to win Pelly's trick challenge!"

"Naughty Fairies for ever!" Nettle
shouted, flitting into a somersault.

"Come on. We have to tell Pelly,"
giggled Tiptoe. "She's judging the trick
challenge this evening. I can't wait to

see her face when she hears this one."

A furry black and yellow bumblebee zoomed down on them with a loud buzz of delight.

"Jeeps, Flea, you need a bath," Kelpie said, wrinkling her nose as the bumblebee butted at her with his furry head. "You smell like a stinkhorn mushroom."

"He's not the only one," said Nettle. She stared at Kelpie's dirty ears.

"I hate baths," Kelpie said. Flea nosed at Kelpie's sticky-looking pocket until she fed him a honeycake. "They're so . . . *wet*."

In the school courtyard, there were still five dandelion seeds on the dandelion clock. The Naughty Fairies were just in time for supper.

Looking triumphant, Brilliance pushed her way to the front of the food queue in the Dining Flowerpot. The others followed. A fairy with blonde pompom bunches was helping herself to a plate full of spiced sorrel bread.

"We've won the Bindweed trick challenge, Pelly," said Brilliance. She took a piece of Pelly's sorrel bread.

Pelly added a roasted daisy heart to her teetering plate. "Don't be so confident, Brilliance," she said. "Onion and Vetch—"

"Put an aphid in Bindweed's mouth, we know," said Nettle. "Big deal."

A tiny green aphid popped its head out of Sesame's top pocket and bleated.

"Not you, Nipper," said Sesame, fondly patting the aphid's head. The aphid disappeared again.

"And Marigold's trick went wrong," added Kelpie. "Bindweed woke up."

"Our trick is totally the best," Brilliance boasted.

"You know the rules, Brilliance," said Pelly, walking towards a table where three fairies with brown, pink and green hair were already sitting. For a St Juniper's pupil, Pelly was surprisingly keen on rules. "We need proof."

CRASH!

Brilliance gave a brilliant smile as Bindweed stormed into the Dining Flowerpot. The garden pixie's feet were leaving a trail of snail slime across the floor and there was a bruise on the end of his nose.

"There you go," said Ping. "Proof.

Move up, Marigold."

Ping plonked her plate next to the fairy with brown hair. Sesame put Nipper the aphid under the table and gave him a cress leaf to chew. And along with all the other fairies at St Juniper's, the Naughty Fairies settled back to watch the show.

Up at the teachers' table, Lord Gallivant the butterfly-riding teacher was fussing over a splodge of daisy gravy on his pale blue tunic.

Dame Honey the Fairy English teacher and Dame Taffeta the Fairy Science teacher were both staring at the ceiling and trying not to giggle.

Dame Lacewing, Deputy Head of St Juniper's, was twirling her splinter spoon thoughtfully between her long fingers.

And Legless, the school earthworm, was sniffing at the snail slime on Bindweed's feet.

Enthralled, the Naughty Fairies watched the garden pixie slam his fists down on the table and growl something furious at the large fairy sitting in the middle. None of the fairies had ever heard the garden pixie speak. They strained to listen, but no one could understand a word.

As they watched, Bindweed turned

around and marched out of the flowerpot again, skidding on the snail slime as he went.

All the fairies in the room started chattering.

Dame Fuddle looked perplexed. She cleared her throat and stood up.

"My dear young fairies!" she said, adjusting her spectacles. "Bindweed

has brought something of a worrying nature to my attention! Someone has played a most unpleasant joke on him today!"

Dame Fuddle always spoke in exclamation marks. The Naughty Fairies sat up straight and tried to look good. Dame Lacewing stared at them with a frown on her face.

"What was the prank, Dame Fuddle?" called a fairy from the back of the flowerpot.

"I won't go into detail!" said Dame Fuddle with dignity. "But it involved a snail, a door and a bruise!"

There was laughter. Under the table, Brilliance gave her friends low fives.

"Our dear garden pixie has made it clear that he will not tolerate another joke!" Dame Fuddle continued. "Apparently there have been several pranks played on him this week! I find it hard to believe that you dear young fairies would play unkind tricks upon your teachers . . ."

Dame Lacewing snorted.

". . . but Bindweed assures me that it is true!" Dame Fuddle gave a delicate cough. "And what is more, he has said that he will leave the school if these pranks do not stop!"

"Leave?" Brilliance said in amazement, her spiced sorrel bread halfway to her mouth.

"Bindweed's been here longer than most of the flowerpots," said Kelpie. She ran her finger around the edge of her plate and licked it. Then she put the plate down on the ground for Flea.

"He'll never go," said Nettle confidently.

"Shh," said Tiptoe. "Dame Fuddle's still talking."

"If we discover the culprits, they will have detention with Bindweed himself for three weeks!" Dame Fuddle concluded. She sat down again. A few fairies applauded. It wasn't clear if they were clapping Dame Fuddle or the snail prank.

"OK," said Pelly in a business-like voice. She pulled out a piece of petal paper and a splinter pencil. "Details."

"We parked a snail in front of Bindweed's door and he ran into it," said Nettle.

Flea buzzed proudly from beneath Kelpie's feet. His furry face was covered in daisy gravy.

"Beat that," said Kelpie.

"Phew," Onion said, pulling back. She waved her hand in front of her face, which was nearly as green as her hair. "When was the last time you had a bath, Kelpie?"

"Don't change the subject," said Kelpie, wagging her finger at Onion. "What are you writing, Pelly?"

The Naughty Fairies leaned over and stared at the paper in front of Pelly. She had made three columns entitled *Rate of Difficulty*, *Originality* and *Effect*.

"You're doing this properly, aren't you?" said Ping.

"Bindweed deserves the best," said Pelly with a nasty grin. That detention was gross."

"So how many points do we get?" Brilliance asked.

"Six for Rate of Difficulty," said Pelly.

"Only six?" said Sesame crossly. "That shell would have been faster without the snail. It took *ages* to get into position."

"Six," said Pelly firmly. She wrote '6' in the *Rate of Difficulty* column. "Eight for Originality," she continued, "and seven for Effect. That gives you a total of . . . thirty-one."

"Twenty-one," Ping corrected. She was better at Maths than Pelly.

"What did the others get?" Brilliance asked with interest.

"Twelve," Marigold mumbled. "It was going well until Bindweed woke up."

Vetch peered out from beneath her pink fringe and grinned, while Onion looked smug.

"Vetch and I got twenty-one as well," Onion said. "It's a draw."

"We can't have a draw!" said Kelpie.

"There's only one thing for it,"

Brilliance said. "Marigold's out. So Onion and Vetch, and us Naughty Fairies, should do one more trick each."

"Fine by us," said Onion.

Vetch nodded.

Pelly put her petal paper in her pocket. "One more trick each," she agreed. "And then we'll have a winner!"

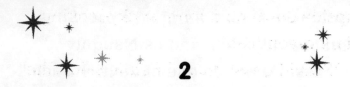

2

A Sticky Situation

Kelpie had got up early to practise flying in the pale dawn light. She'd only just learned to fly, and the twirling and floating was still a wonderful new feeling.

"Straight up . . ." Kelpie pushed off the ground, for a mid-air somersault that Nettle had shown her. "Over," she added, flicking her legs up and round. "And down again. Oh, *great*," she murmured, staring at the puddle of bird poo now covering her feet.

Flea whizzed into a somersault as well. Somehow, it went wrong. Kelpie put her hands on her hips and stared at the bumblebee, who was hanging upside down on a long, sticky-looking, dark green leaf.

"Stupid goosegrass," Kelpie said. She tried to pull her bumblebee off the goosegrass leaf. Flea strained and puffed, eager to help but making things worse. "Horrible, sticky—"

Kelpie suddenly gasped as she thought of something.

"Come on, Flea!" She grabbed a handful of Flea's fur and tugged one last time. Flea came away from the leaf with a ripping sound. "We have to get to breakfast – now!"

*

"Naughty Fairies!" Kelpie ran into the Dining Flowerpot and thumped her fist on the bark table. Her five friends jumped out of their skins.

"Kelpie!" Brilliance said, nearly choking on her elderberry juice. "What's the hurry?"

"That's what I'm trying to tell you," said Kelpie. "Naughty Fairies!"

This was their fairy code.

"OK," sighed Nettle. "Me first. Um . . . nitwit forget-me-not." She put her fist on top of Kelpie's.

Sesame wrinkled her nose. "Nipper farted." The aphid in her top pocket gave a wriggle.

"Good one, Sesame," said Tiptoe. "And you spelled it right for once. Go on, put your hand on Nettle's."

"No," Sesame said. "Nipper really did just fart."

"Well, it fits," said Ping. "Not fair."

"Either it fits, or it's not fair," said

22

Tiptoe patiently. "I – oh." She looked sheepish. "Not fair – NF. OK, how about . . . niggle fig?"

"Nosey flamingos," said Brilliance. "Fly, fly . . ."

"To the SKY!" The Naughty Fairies threw their fists in the air.

"I have got the best trick," Kelpie said, plonking herself down at the table.

"You reek," said Brilliance. "What is that smell?"

Kelpie looked down at herself. "A mixture of bird poo and aphid fart."

"Not to mention basic dirt," added Ping. "You've *got* to have a bath, Kelpie."

"Like a bath matters right now." Kelpie said. "I've got a fantastic trick we can play on Bindweed to win Pelly's challenge!"

"Ooh!" said Sesame, leaning forward. "Does it involve bird poo?"

Kelpie shook her head. "Let's meet up at the Hedge straight after Wing and Wand Care," she said. "We'll blow Onion and Vetch out of the water!"

"On the subject of water," Brilliance began. Kelpie smacked her.

Wand and Wing Care was the Naughty Fairies' favourite lesson. No one listened to anything Dame Fuddle said, and Dame Fuddle never noticed.

"Today we are looking at our wands!"

24

Dame Fuddle announced, as the class
milled around the courtyard.

"We thought it might be wands today,
Dame Fuddle," said Ping.

"Or maybe wings," added Brilliance.

"Do you ever wonder how to obtain a
high shine on your wands?" Dame
Fuddle asked, beaming at the class. She
waved her own wand at the fairies. It
gleamed in the morning light.

"No," said Kelpie, taking out her wand and studying it. She had painted it black and yellow in honour of Flea. It wasn't very clean, and it certainly wasn't very shiny. "But I do sometimes wonder how it works."

"Let me share a secret with you!" Dame Fuddle said. She swished her wand through the air, spelling the word BEES in a shiny ribbon of fire.

Kelpie looked interested. "Now we're talking," she said. Bees were Kelpie's favourite subject.

"Bees produce wax!" Dame Fuddle continued.

"So do my ears," said Ping. "Do you think Dame Fuddle would notice if I left? I want to fly Pong."

Dame Fuddle gave a little skip. "Beeswax and lavender and a dash of magic!" she warbled.

"Dashing would be good," Sesame whispered. "Dashing right out of here.

If Ping's going to fly Pong, I want to fly Sulphur." Sulphur was Sesame's Brimstone butterfly.

"Let's collect our ingredients, fairies!" Dame Fuddle called, with a clap of her hands. "Kelpie dear? Could Flea spare us a little waxy-woo?"

At the mention of his name, Flea buzzed down from his sunny spot on the roof of the Butterfly Stables.

"Ah, Fleazle-weazle," Dame Fuddle crooned, tickling Flea under the chin. Several fairies sniggered. "Some waxy-woo for Dame Fuddly-wuddly?"

"I think I'm going to be sick," said Kelpie.

Flea raised one waxy leg in the air and Dame Fuddle carefully scraped at his knee.

"You will find lavender growing beside the Butterfly Stables!" Dame Fuddle twittered, putting her beeswax into a walnut-shell cauldron. "When

you've collected some petals, we will combine our ingredients! And then comes the fun part!" She twinkled at the class. *The magic words!"*

"Ooh," said Nettle with a yawn. "Can't wait."

Clattering and shoving and shouting, the fairies wandered around the courtyard poking at the weeds.

"Lavender!" Dame Fuddle shouted hopefully. "Nothing else will do!"

Armfuls of the wrong-coloured petals were dumped beside Dame Fuddle's walnut-shell cauldron by chatting fairies. As the pile grew higher, even Dame Fuddle's smile began to wobble.

When she saw Nettle carrying a single purple lavender petal towards her, the head teacher almost burst into song.

"Exactly right, Nettle dear!" she trilled. "You're a credit to the class!"

Dame Fuddle dropped the lavender

into the cauldron of melted beeswax.
A delicious smell wafted through
the air.

"Good enough to eat," Tiptoe said.
"Hey, does anyone have a dew chew?"

"Stir, stir, stir!" said Dame Fuddle.
She tried to make her eyes look round
and spooky as she stirred the melting
wax. Several fairies lay down in the
middle of the courtyard and started
sunbathing. The chatter got louder as
Dame Fuddle ladled a small amount of
the mixture into an acorn cup.

"*Lavandula angustifolia!*" Dame
Fuddle sang, brandishing her wand
above her acorn cup. She spun the
words out: *Lavannnnndula
angustifooolia.* "*Bombus hortorum!
Mico!*"

The acorn cup flashed and gleamed.
A couple of fairies oohed dramatically,
and Dame Fuddle flushed pink with
pride and pleasure.

The head teacher then divided the class into groups. Each group was given an acorn cup full of lavender wax and a set of instructions.

"Try the words!" Dame Fuddle said, springing nimbly among her chatting pupils. "Lav*annnn*dula angusti*fool*ia! Lav*annn*dula!"

"Lavvy doodaa angry fooled ya," Brilliance said. She poked the Naughty Fairies' acorn cup with the tip of her grubby wand.

"Cute," said Sesame.

They all stared at the tiny blue frog which had appeared in the acorn cup.

"Not quite!" Dame Fuddle said encouragingly. "But a jolly good try!"

As Sesame reached for the frog, it burped and disappeared in a puff of smoke.

Somewhere behind them, a bluebell started ringing. Dame Fuddle looked disappointed. "Alas!" she said. "Out of

time, out of time! Clear away now, my
dear fairies – and don't forget the magic
words! A fairy's wand can never, ever
be too shiny!"

Nettle spat on her wand and shined
it on her oak-leaf trousers. She stared at
it carefully. "Looks all right to me,"
she said.

"We've just got time to do my trick
before Fairy Maths," Kelpie said, as the

fairies wandered into the playground for their mid-morning break. Flea buzzed high above their heads. "We need goosegrass. Try not to get stuck to it, OK?"

The Naughty Fairies trailed off to the large patch of goosegrass beside the Hedge, where Flea had got stuck earlier that morning. Watching from a safe distance, Flea zoomed into a series of loops above the cobweb trampoline.

By wrapping their hands deep in their sleeves, the fairies managed to pull a long, thin goosegrass leaf off its stem. The sticky bits glistened in the sun.

"There's Bindweed," Tiptoe hissed suddenly, as they carried the sticky leaf past the school's glass-jar greenhouse. "Act normal."

The Naughty Fairies dropped the leaf like it was red-hot. They put bright smiles on their faces. Brilliance gave a little wave.

A few paces ahead of them, Bindweed was tying his team of leaf-cutter ants to the twig-mower. The ants pawed the ground, eyeing the long Sports Field grass with enthusiasm. Bindweed leaned back on the mower and stared at the fairies sourly.

"Lovely morning for a bit of mowing," said Kelpie.

Bindweed grunted. Hitching up his leaf-mould trousers, he turned his back and shuffled into his flowerpot. The

ants tugged restlessly at the mower.

"We've got about half a dandelion
seed," said Kelpie, turning to the others.
"Wrap the goosegrass round the handles
of the mower as quickly as you can. Go!"

They picked up the goosegrass and
rushed towards the ants. The nearest
ant growled and waggled its antennae
at them.

"Won't Bindweed notice?" Tiptoe
asked nervously as they wound the
goosegrass leaf tightly into position.

"By the time he notices, he'll be stuck to the handles," Kelpie said with confidence.

"Ow!" Nettle yelled. She grabbed her leg where the growling ant had bitten her. "Stupid, shiny-headed—"

"Shut *up*, Nettle!" Ping hissed.

It was too late. Bindweed had put his head out of his flowerpot.

"Run!" Brilliance squealed.

As the Naughty Fairies raced to get away, Tiptoe tripped and fell against the mower. Putting her hands out to save herself, she landed squarely on the mower handles.

Bindweed gave a crow of triumph and pounced as Tiptoe tried to free herself. Tiptoe wept and struggled. The other Naughty Fairies slowed to a very reluctant halt.

"There's been a mistake," Brilliance said. She gave Bindweed her most brilliant smile.

Bindweed narrowed his eyes and
pointed a long gnarly finger at
Brilliance. The Naughty Fairies flinched
at his expression of fury, and even
Brilliance blinked a bit.

Then, without a word, the old pixie
turned and marched off the Sports
Field, towards the Nettle Patch and out
of sight.

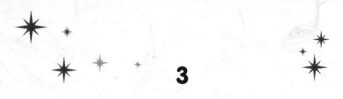

3

Gone!

"Whoops," said Kelpie.

Tiptoe was still struggling to pull her hands away from the sticky twig-mower handle.

"Bindweed's gone," Nettle said in amazement.

"*Gone* gone?" Brilliance asked. "Or just I'll-be-back-later gone?"

The leaf-cutter ants chewed grass and wriggled in their twig-mower harnesses. The ant which had bitten Nettle stared at her with flinty ant eyes.

"Oh well," said Ping. "At least he won't be here to take the detention."

"What detention?" Kelpie challenged. "No one knows he's gone yet."

"Or why," Nettle added.

"Maybe he won't be missed," said Tiptoe hopefully.

Sesame nodded. "It's not like he does anything useful," she said. "I mean, how hard is it to cut the grass?"

The Naughty Fairies felt better.

The bad-tempered ant lunged at Nettle's leg again.

"Let's go back," said Nettle. "Before that ant bites my leg off."

"We should unharness the ants," said Sesame. "We can't leave them out here all day."

"Why not?" Kelpie asked.

"It's *cruel*," said Sesame. Sesame loved all insects, big and small. "They need to be groomed and fed and watered. Like butterflies."

A small leaf-cutter ant at the back of the team lifted its head and squealed.

"I think that one's missing Bindweed already," said Tiptoe.

"We have to go back," Nettle insisted. "We're late for our next lesson. It's going to look very suspicious if we go missing at the same time as Bindweed."

"OK," said Sesame, looking anxiously at the team of ants. "But we have to tell someone that Bindweed's gone. Otherwise these ants will be left here too long."

"Let's tell Dame Honey," Ping suggested. Dame Honey was everyone's favourite teacher. It was always easy giving her bad news.

"Tell Dame Honey what, precisely?"

Dame Lacewing was leaning against the cobweb trampoline and looking at them with interest. Her pet beetle, Pipsqueak, stood at her feet.

"Oh no," Ping groaned.

"Oops," croaked Sesame, clutching Nipper the aphid tightly to her chest.

"Quite," said Dame Lacewing.

Tall and dark and fierce, Dame

Lacewing could spot a prank almost before it happened.

Brilliance found a brilliant smile from somewhere. "Hello, Dame Lacewing," she said. "What are you doing here?"

Dame Lacewing looked down her long nose at the fairies. "Fairy Maths started five dandelion seeds ago. I thought I would come and . . . hunt you down."

She smiled in a spidery way that

made the Naughty Fairies feel like six
fat flies.

"And here we are," said Brilliance.
"What a coincidence."

Tiptoe quietly tried to unstick herself
from the mower handles. Dame
Lacewing swung round to her at once.
"What are you doing, Tiptoe?" she
snapped. "What are these ants doing in
harness? Where is Bindweed?"

"In his flowerpot," said Kelpie.

"In the Strawberry Patch," said
Nettle, at the same time.

"Really," said Dame Lacewing.

Pipsqueak sniffed at the goosegrass
on the mower handles while Tiptoe
stared unhappily at her feet.

"So when I saw Bindweed marching
through the Nettle Patch just now,
looking like thunder," Dame Lacewing
continued, "I was imagining things?"

Even Brilliance couldn't think of a
reply to that.

Dame Lacewing pointed her wand at Tiptoe. "Galium aparine."

The goosegrass slid away from the mower handles and piled into a heap on the grass.

"I want you all inside at *once*," Dame Lacewing said, tucking her wand into her cobweb-silk gown. "If Bindweed has left St Juniper's on account of your latest prank, you are in Very Deep Trouble Indeed."

"I don't see why," said Ping sulkily. "What does Bindweed *do*, anyway?"

"Anyone can mow the stupid grass," Tiptoe said.

"He doesn't teach any lessons," added Sesame.

"He hardly ever smiles," said Nettle.

"And he doesn't even *speak*," said Kelpie. "At least, not to us."

"I mean," said Brilliance with a shrug, "who's going to miss him?"

An interesting expression flitted

across Dame Lacewing's face. It was as if she couldn't decide whether to eat up the fairies straight away or save them for later.

"You'll find a list of Bindweed's chores pinned up in his flowerpot," she said. "Come to my office when you've finished."

Dame Lacewing clicked her tongue at Pipsqueak and strode back towards the school.

"What's that funny rumbling noise?" Tiptoe asked.

"I think Dame Lacewing is laughing," said Brilliance doubtfully.

The Naughty Fairies watched the Fairy Maths teacher disappear inside one of the classroom flowerpots.

"Is that our detention?" Nettle said at last. "Doing Bindweed's poxy chores?"

"Snipping a bit of grass," said Kelpie.

"Sweeping up a bit of ant poo," said Brilliance.

"Snoring," said Ping.

The Naughty Fairies giggled.

"Let's go and find this list," said Tiptoe. "If we do it right, we'll miss the rest of Fairy Maths and be in perfect time for lunch."

Bindweed's flowerpot was mossy and cool. It was furnished with a chair, a table and a bed, some shelves and a large noticeboard. Everything was made out of a woody, squashy material that the Naughty Fairies had never seen before.

"What is this stuff?" Tiptoe asked, pressing her finger down on the woody-looking table.

"Cork," said Ping knowledgeably. "Humans put it in bottles of fizzy stuff to stop the fizz getting out."

"So where did Bindweed get it?" Brilliance asked.

Nobody knew the answer to that.

Kelpie sat down on a broken-looking cork chair, and the Naughty Fairies looked at the large cork noticeboard beside the door. The list of Bindweed's chores was pinned up exactly where Dame Lacewing had said it would be.

A Very. Long. List. Indeed.

"Bindweed does all *that*?" said Brilliance. "Every day?"

Tiptoe took down the list. The petal paper trailed down to her feet. The Naughty Fairies gathered round.

"Feed the ants," Tiptoe began.

"Water, groom and stable them," Sesame added, reading over Tiptoe's shoulder.

"Mow the Sports Field," Tiptoe continued. "Trim the Nettle Patch and the Hedge Tunnel. Weed the courtyard."

"Wash down the flowerpots," Nettle read. "Mend the cobweb trampoline."

"Fill walnut-shell washbasins with rainwater," Brilliance said.

"And tend the glass-jar greenhouse,"
finished Ping.

The Naughty Fairies all sat down
together, very suddenly, on the floor of
Bindweed's flowerpot.

"There's six of us," said Nettle
bravely. "We'll do it."

"Maybe we'll be finished by sunset,"
Sesame said.

Nipper the aphid bleated sadly from
deep inside Sesame's pocket.

Kelpie looked at Tiptoe. "Are you OK?"

Tiptoe looked like she was going to
burst. "By . . . by sunset?" she said. Her
bottom lip wobbled. "But – that means
we'll have to miss *lunch*!"

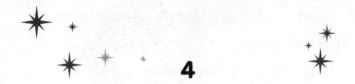

4

A Not So Brilliant Plan

A very sorry huddle of Naughty Fairies limped back into St Juniper's at sunset.

"I hate ants," Nettle moaned. She rubbed at the bite marks on her arms and legs. "They've got teeth *everywhere*."

Brilliance stared at her soggy feet. "These were my best starflower slippers," she grumbled. "I got more water on me than I got in all the walnut-shell washbasins put together."

"The cobweb trampoline had a thousand holes in it," Ping complained. "I mended at *least* nine hundred and ninety-nine."

"The Nettle Patch stung my bottom,"

said Sesame mournfully.

"I thought it was OK," said Tiptoe.

"That's because you got the glass-jar greenhouse," said Kelpie. Flea rubbed his furry head against her knees. "You just sat there and ate the blackcurrants."

"I did *not*," Tiptoe said.

"Yes you did," said Nettle.

"Well," said Tiptoe after a pause. "I might have eaten one. Or maybe two."

Brilliance pulled off her starflower slippers with a squelch. "I suppose we should go and see Dame Lacewing," she said gloomily.

"You'd better have a wash first," Kelpie told Tiptoe. "You've got blackcurrant juice behind your ears."

"You can't talk," Ping said. "You've got more dirt on you than a dung beetle."

"This isn't dirt," said Kelpie,

admiring the new layer of mud on her hands. "It's camouflage."

Dame Lacewing's study was in a tall, neat flowerpot near the Watering Can. Pipsqueak the beetle was in his usual place beside the fire, snoring gently.

"So," said Dame Lacewing as the Naughty Fairies stood in a line in front of her desk. "Did you enjoy doing nothing today?"

"Yes thanks, Dame Lacewing," said Ping.

"Glad to hear it," said Dame Lacewing. "So you won't mind doing it again tomorrow."

"Tomorrow!" the Naughty Fairies gasped together.

"And the day after that," Dame Lacewing continued. "And again and again until either Bindweed returns, or we find a new garden pixie to take over his duties. Here is the Fairy Maths work that you missed." She handed out six dried seedpods and six pieces of petal paper. "Have it on my desk tomorrow morning after breakfast. That will be all."

The Naughty Fairies trailed out into the darkening courtyard.

"Homework *and* more chores," said Sesame miserably. "I think I'm going to cry."

Nettle looked at her seedpod. "What do we do with these?" she asked.

"Open the pod," said Kelpie, reading

from her piece of petal paper. "Count and weigh the seeds, then calculate the total pod weight."

Tiptoe gulped. She wasn't very good at Fairy Maths.

"No way," said Sesame.

"No *weigh*," Ping said. "Get it?"

"This is no laughing matter," said Brilliance as they walked into their dormitory. "I have a *brilliant* plan—"

"Which you'll tell us tomorrow morning," Kelpie interrupted. "I want to go to bed."

"Don't you mean, you want to have a *bath*?" said Brilliance.

Kelpie ignored Brilliance and pulled off her boots.

"Por!"

"Euw!"

"Yuk!"

The Naughty Fairies held their noses at the smell of Kelpie's feet.

"Night," said Kelpie, climbing into

her foxglove sleeping bag.

"What about the seedpod homework?" Sesame said.

"My seedpod weighs twenty-three kilosquirts," said Kelpie.

"Wow," Tiptoe said, looking impressed. "Is that right?"

"How would I know?" Kelpie demanded. "I just made it up. Go to sleep, everyone. We've got work tomorrow."

Because they were so tired, the Naughty Fairies overslept. And because they overslept, once again Kelpie had no time for a bath.

"You really do stink now, Kelpie," said Ping in disgust. "You're practically putting Tiptoe off her breakfast."

Tiptoe looked up from her bowl of rosebud muesli. "What?"

"If Flea can live with the smell, so can you," said Kelpie, pouring out a glass of

strawberry squash. Flea laid his head
on Kelpie's feet and looked up
adoringly at her.

"What's your brilliant plan then,
Brilliance?" Sesame asked. Nipper the
aphid was curled up on her lap.

Brilliance put her fist on the table.
"Naughty Fairies," she announced.

"Just tell us," Kelpie growled.

"We don't have time for NFing now,"
said Nettle.

Brilliance looked annoyed. "OK," she said at last. "Job combining."

"Great!" said Tiptoe. "Um – what does that mean?"

Brilliance explained. "By combining jobs, we can get everything done in half the time. Three of Bindweed's jobs use water, right?"

Nettle checked the jobs off on her fingers. "Washing the flowerpots, filling the walnut-shell washbasins, watering the greenhouse."

"Don't forget the ants," Sesame put in. "They need water too."

"Like I'm going to forget the ants," Nettle muttered, examining an ant bite on the back of her hand.

"So," Brilliance continued. "We do all the jobs at once. Rig up a tube from the Watering Can, and we're done."

Everyone had to admit that Brilliance's idea did sound brilliant.

"What about weeding the

greenhouse?" Tiptoe asked.

"And feeding the ants?" Sesame added.

Brilliance waved her hand in the air. "Shut the ants in the greenhouse. They can eat the weeds. Two jobs at once."

Brilliance's job combining was sounding better and better.

"That just leaves the trimming, the mowing and the last hole in the cobweb trampoline," said Ping. "And we did the mowing yesterday."

The Naughty Fairies felt much more cheerful.

"I mean," said Brilliance grandly. "What can possibly go wrong?"

Now they had a plan, the Naughty Fairies were keen to get started. They even had time to stick their tongues out at the fairies who were filing off to Fairy Science. After handing in their Fairy Maths homework and shutting the ants in the glass-jar greenhouse, they flew

out of the school courtyard towards the
Watering Can.

The Watering Can was so high that
none of the fairies had ever seen the top
of it. It glistened with rust and slugs,
and damp grass grew around its base.

Brilliance pointed at a long, knobbly
stick that lay propped up against the
Watering Can. "Look," she said in a
pleased voice. "A tube."

"It's a stick," said Nettle. "It's not
a tube."

"Don't be so sure," said Brilliance.
"It's one of those stick tubes that
Humans grow peas on."

Sure enough, the long knobbly stick
had a hole running through the middle
of it.

"How do we get it into the water?"
Tiptoe asked.

"And how do we get the water into *it*?"
added Nettle.

It was a challenge. The Naughty

Fairies scratched their heads and tried
to remember a spell that would help.

"We could try a come-to-me charm,"
suggested Kelpie.

They had learned come-to-me charms
during Ping's first term at St Juniper's.

"We've never tried a come-to-me
charm on something that big," said
Nettle doubtfully.

"How do come-to-me charms work?"
Sesame asked. "I can never remember."

"You measure the thing, multiply the
wotsit and say the magic word," said
Brilliance. "Easy."

The fairies measured the peastick.
The stick was five hundred and fifty-
five millisquirts long and twenty
millisquirts wide.

"We've got to multiply five hundred
and fifty-five by twenty?" Tiptoe said in
horror. "Five hundred and fifty-five has
got three fives in it. I can only multiply
by one."

64

"I counted all the hairs on Flea's tummy once," said Kelpie. "It took practically the whole of Fairy Science. I only lost count twice."

"Hello? This is multiplying, not adding," said Brilliance.

"It's impossible," Nettle said. "We'll have to think of another way."

"I can multiply it," said Ping loftily.

"OK," Kelpie challenged. "Prove it."

"One million, one hundred and ten thousand," said Ping.

There was an impressed silence.

Ping swished her wand around. "Shall I do the magic words as well?" she asked.

"I suppose," Brilliance said, a little grumpily. "Since you've got your wand out."

Ping sprang off the ground, whirring her wings. Higher and higher she flew, until she was floating high above the Watering Can. She twirled her magic

wand, printing *1110000* on to the air in
a squiggle of fire.

"*Andeca!*" she shouted.

"The peastick's not moving," Tiptoe
said after a moment.

"No," said Sesame in a trembling voice. "But something else is!"

And as they watched, the Watering Can heaved into the air.

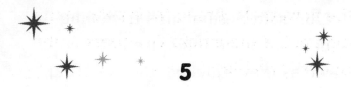

5

Water Water Everywhere

A torrent of stinking brown water shot from the spout of the Watering Can and swooshed through the flowerpots of St Juniper's. Weeds were ripped from the ground. The dandelion clock in the courtyard snapped in half. Fairies came shrieking out of

the flowerpots, lifting their petal skirts
high out of the muck. The doors of the
Butterfly Stables
banged open,
and a stream
of panicking
butterflies

took to the skies with damp wings. Within moments, the whole of St Juniper's was transformed into a smelly brown puddle.

"I think," said Ping, "that maybe I added too many noughts to that sum."

"Easy mistake," said Tiptoe.

"At least we won't have to wash down the flowerpots," said Kelpie.

"Or do the weeding," added Brilliance.

"Shame the water didn't hit you, Kelpie," said Nettle. "It's smelly, but not nearly as smelly as you."

"Dame Lacewing is going to kill us," Sesame moaned. She clutched Nipper so tightly that the aphid made a noise like a deflating balloon.

"Scatter," Brilliance ordered.

The Naughty Fairies didn't need to be told twice. As the Watering Can teetered and wobbled back into position, they fled.

*

The atmosphere in the Dining Flowerpot that evening was tense. The floor was a sea of sticky mud, and the smell of stagnant water hung in the air like smoke.

"Grass salad," said Tiptoe, poking at her leaf plate. "How's a fairy supposed to survive on grass salad?"

"We're lucky to get it," said Nettle.

Flea stared forlornly at the grass stem Kelpie had given him to chew.

" 'Let's shut the ants in the greenhouse'," Kelpie mimicked, glaring at Brilliance as she prodded a dry-looking piece of grass. " 'They can eat the weeds.' "

"The weeds, the plants, the fruit," said Sesame.

Nipper gave a tragic squeak.

"Everything, basically," added Ping.

"I like grass salad," said Brilliance defiantly. She picked up a pale green frond and chewed it with determination.

"This is all your fault, Brilliance," Kelpie hissed. "We're on night detention, scrubbing the floors in the whole school because of you."

"*And* we've got to do it on empty stomachs," said Tiptoe.

"*And* we've still got Bindweed's

normal chores to do," Ping put in.

Sesame nodded. "Not to mention all the extra homework for the lessons we're missing. How much worse can this get?"

Someone tapped Brilliance on the shoulder.

"The trick challenge is cancelled," Pelly said as she passed their table. "The rules are that we can't do tricks if Bindweed's not here. So it's a draw."

The Naughty Fairies groaned.

"So all this trouble's been for nothing?" Ping complained.

"Keep your wings on, everybody," said Brilliance. "I've got a brilliant plan."

"NO," said Kelpie loudly. "No more brilliant plans."

"So you want to keep doing Bindweed's chores for ever, do you?" Brilliance demanded. "Stabling smelly ants? Doing night detentions on your hands and knees? Making up answers to homework?"

"We do that anyway," Tiptoe said.

"You've *got* to hear my brilliant plan," said Brilliance stubbornly. "You don't have any choice. Naughty Fairies!"

After a moment, the others reluctantly put their fists on hers.

"Nightmare freak."

"Nodding flannel."

"Nippy flicker."

"Gnat fruit!"

"Gnat's spelt with a G, Sesame," Nettle said. "You're so rubbish at spelling. Nelly firecracker."

"Fly, fly – to the SKY!"

The Naughty Fairies threw their fists into the air.

"Here's the plan." Brilliance swallowed her grass stalk and patted her mouth. "We find Bindweed tonight and bring him back."

"How?" Kelpie demanded. "He could

be anywhere."

Brilliance fluttered her wings. "Remember these?" she said. "Bindweed's on foot. We'll find him in half a dandelion seed if we look."

"What about our detention?" Sesame asked.

"We'll just get another one tomorrow," Brilliance said. "If we find Bindweed

tonight, at least we won't have his
chores as well. We'll make a break for it
when the teachers leave the flowerpot."

The Naughty Fairies munched their
grass salad and waited for their chance.
It almost didn't come.

"You six will come straight to my
study for your night detention when
you've washed your hands," Dame
Lacewing said, stopping at the Naughty
Fairies' table on her way out. "And
Kelpie – do something about the dirt on
your face. You resemble a clod of mud
which happens to have wings."

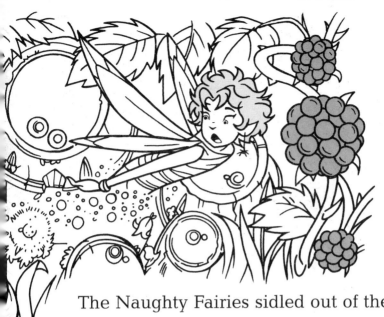

The Naughty Fairies sidled out of the
flowerpot with the rest of the school.
Then, after checking for teachers, they
rose into the air with Flea close behind
them.

"Higher!" shouted Nettle, as they
flew up towards the darkening sky.
"High as you can!"

"Ooh," Sesame moaned, beating her
wings hard as the flowerpot towers of St
Juniper's shrank away beneath them.
"I've never been this high before."

Nipper the aphid put his head out of
Sesame's pocket. He took one look at

the long drop to the ground, and was
horribly sick.

"Lovely," said Kelpie, wiping at the
smudge of sick which had landed on
her sleeve. "Thanks, Nipper."

Soon, the whole Garden was spread
out below the Naughty Fairies. They
could see the Shed, and the Watering
Can, the cluster of school flowerpots
and the Nettle Patch. The setting sun
caught the Pond, which gleamed like
beaten silver. Flea swooped and
zoomed around the fairies like a black
and yellow powder puff.

"Gotcha!" Brilliance called
triumphantly, after the Naughty Fairies
had been searching the Garden for
several dandelion seeds.

She pointed down at the Pond. The
Naughty Fairies could see what looked
like a fat, windblown autumn leaf
sitting on a little beach.

"It's a leaf," said Sesame.

"I've never seen a leaf holding a fishing rod," said Kelpie.

"Or a leaf scratching its bottom," Nettle added. "It's definitely him. Let's go get him!"

Brilliance pulled in her wings and went into a steep dive, and the others followed. Down, down, down – the Naughty Fairies bounced and spun on the breeze as they sank among the weeds and reeds and grasses at the Pond's edge.

"That was fantastic," Nettle enthused as she landed with Kelpie and Flea.

"Urgh," said Sesame, lifting a very pale green Nipper from her pocket and putting him down on the ground. "I've got aphid sick all over me."

"I – ooph," said Tiptoe, landing on her bottom as Brilliance and Ping came to a graceful halt on a blade of grass beside her.

The setting sun cast deep stripy

shadows on the sand and pebbles around them. Bindweed was hunched over his fishing rod with his back to the Naughty Fairies. He clearly hadn't heard them arrive.

Behind the pixie, the Naughty Fairies could see a little tent made out of an oak leaf and a twig. There was a flickering grass bonfire in front of the tent, and the sweet smouldering remains of a barbecued blackberry.

"What if he doesn't want to come back?" Tiptoe whispered.

"He looks like he's on holiday, doesn't he?" said Nettle.

"No one ever wants to come back from holiday," Ping said.

"He looks happy," said Sesame sadly. "Maybe we will have to do his chores for ever, after all."

"Don't worry," said Brilliance. "I have a brilliant plan."

"Great," Kelpie muttered.

The Naughty Fairies tiptoed along the beach towards the pixie. Bindweed was sitting so still that, for a moment, the fairies wondered if he was real.

Brilliance was just about to tap Bindweed on the shoulder when there was a loud noise overhead.

RRROO! Roo-COO . . .

In a flash, Bindweed had dropped his rod, leaped to his feet and dived into his tent. The whole tent shook like a – well, like a leaf. Which of course, it was.

Flea shuffled a little closer to Kelpie's muddy ankles.

"What was that?" Tiptoe squeaked nervously.

"Just a pigeon," said Ping.

"Fancy being scared of a pigeon," Nettle said.

"Ordinary things can seem scary when you're away from home," said Sesame wisely.

The Naughty Fairies stared at the little fishing rod lying abandoned on the beach. The oak-leaf tent was still shaking.

A slow smile spread across Brilliance's pretty face. "I think," she said, "that my brilliant plan just got brillianter."

"More brilliant," Kelpie corrected.

"You said it." Brilliance stuck out her fist. "Naughty Fairies!"

Half a dandelion passed before Bindweed cautiously came out of his tent. It was nearly dark, and a slice of pale moon hung in the sky. The old pixie stood beside the glowing grass bonfire and stared across the water of the Pond.

The Naughty Fairies watched from high overhead, perching on the tip of a velvety bulrush.

"He still looks nervous," said Kelpie, stroking a snoozing Flea.

"Perfect," said Ping approvingly.

"Got the spider silk, Nettle?" Brilliance asked.

Nettle pulled a ball of spider silk from her pocket. "Right here."

"Clever things," said Tiptoe, reaching out to stroke Nettle's ear spiders. Exhausted by their spinning, both spiders were fast asleep.

"Where's Nipper?" Brilliance asked.

Sesame reluctantly passed Nipper to Brilliance. "I'm not sure this is such a brilliant idea," she began.

Brilliance tied the spider silk neatly around Nipper's tummy. "Nipper hated flying," she said. "This is much kinder than taking him back to St Juniper's with us. We'll lower him until he touches Bindweed's head with his feet. Bindweed will be so scared that he'll run back to St Juniper's without a backward glance, and everything will be back to normal."

"And we'll never have to go near Bindweed's horrible ants again," said Nettle happily.

"I suppose," said Sesame. She kissed the aphid's shiny green head. "Good luck, Nipper," she said. Her eyes looked a bit wet. "Just don't look down."

Ping, Nettle and Tiptoe started lowering Nipper off the bulrush, paying

out the spider silk millisquirt by
millisquirt. Kelpie hung over the edge
of the bulrush and watched. Very
slowly, the little green aphid descended
through the gloom.

"Is Nipper OK?" Sesame asked,
sounding anxious.

"I think he's got his eyes shut," said
Kelpie.

Bindweed was still standing on the
beach with his hands behind his back.

It was hard to tell what he was
thinking.

"Is Nipper nearly there?" Tiptoe
puffed.

Kelpie was quiet for a moment. "It
depends where you mean by 'there',"
she said. "Near Bindweed's tent? Yes.
Near Bindweed? No."

The Naughty Fairies peered down at
Bindweed's silhouette. Kelpie was right.

Nipper was too far from Bindweed.

"Stop," Brilliance commanded.

Ping, Nettle and Tiptoe stopped.
Nipper was left dangling in mid air,
several millisquirts from the target.

"The rope needs a nudge," said
Brilliance. "Kelpie? You're nearest."

Kelpie shuffled a little further off the
bulrush. The spider silk was still out of
reach. Stretching out her hand, Kelpie

managed to bat the silk with her
fingertips.

All at once, three things happened.

Nipper landed on Bindweed's head.

Bindweed bellowed.

And with a slow-motion topple, Kelpie
fell off the bulrush.

"Whoaaaa!" Kelpie shouted, trying to unfurl her wings in time.

"Waaah?" Bindweed yelled, staring around in a wild kind of way.

"Kelpie just landed in the Pond!"
Tiptoe squealed, as the Naughty Fairies
rushed to peer over the edge of the
bulrush.

"Just look at Bindweed go," said Ping
with satisfaction, as the old pixie

hitched up his leaf-mould trousers and sprinted for the Nettle Patch and St Juniper's as fast as his short legs could carry him.

Nipper scurried off and Flea buzzed anxiously overhead as Kelpie rose to the surface of the Pond and spluttered in the moonlight.

"And thank Nature," said Brilliance. "Kelpie's had a bath at last."

6

Down With A Bump

The Naughty Fairies kept their heads down the following day.

This was surprisingly easy to do, as Dame Lacewing was away. And although the brimming walnut-shell washbasins and polished flowerpot floors pointed to the fact that the pixie had returned, there had also been no sign of Bindweed. The Naughty Fairies were keen to keep out of his way. Particularly as polishing the floors had been part of the night detention they had missed.

Fairy Sports was the first lesson of the day, with trampolining to start with and flying races to finish. A fairy with blonde pompom bunches bounced past the Naughty Fairies as they trooped towards the Sports Field.

"Hey, Pelly!" Brilliance called. "You know the trick challenge?"

"I cancelled it, remember?" Pelly said.

"But Bindweed's back now," said Brilliance persuasively.

"We found him," said Nettle.

"And boy, did we trick him," said Ping, sounding gleeful.

"Want to hear the details?" Kelpie raised her eyebrows.

Pelly shook her head.

"But we did trick him," Tiptoe insisted.

"And guess what? He didn't even realise!" Sesame giggled.

"If he didn't realise," Pelly pointed out, "then he's not going to complain about it to Dame Fuddle, is he? So where's your proof?"

The Naughty Fairies were silent.

"But that's not *fair*," Brilliance protested.

"Sorry," said Pelly. "But those are the rules. Onion and Vetch have agreed to a draw anyway. Unless you can do a trick *with proof* in the next five dandelion seeds, the challenge is over."

"I hate rules," Kelpie said in disgust as Pelly ran on.

"We didn't do that trick on Bindweed to win the trick challenge," Sesame pointed out. "We did it to get him back, and it worked. We can't have everything."

They rounded the replanted glass-jar greenhouse and the cobweb trampoline came into view. Bindweed was bouncing on it with a look of gloomy concentration on his face.

"What's Bindweed doing?" Tiptoe asked curiously.

"Testing for holes," Nettle guessed.

The fairies stood around the

trampoline in groups and waited for Dame Taffeta, who taught Fairy Sports. No one paid the trampolining Bindweed much attention. It was amazing how quickly things had gone back to normal.

There was a sudden cheering noise from the House and a loud *pop*. The fairies jumped out of their skins as something whistled over their heads and landed beside Bindweed's flowerpot. Bindweed turned his head in mid-bounce, and fell through a hole in the trampoline.

"Remember that thousandth hole I never got round to mending?" said Ping, as everyone rushed to help the dazed-looking pixie to his feet. "I think Bindweed just found it."

Pelly dashed up to them. "Did you do that?" she demanded.

"It wasn't totally on purpose," Sesame began. "OW!"

"Of course we did," said Brilliance, taking her foot off Sesame's toe.

"Congratulations," Pelly said. "Everyone saw it, which counts as proof. You just won the challenge."

"Brilliant," said Brilliance blissfully. "What was that flying thing anyway?"

Tiptoe asked, staring at the strange
object lying beside Bindweed's front
door.

"That," said Ping, "was a cork."

Kelpie grinned. "I think Bindweed
just got himself a new chair."

An Utter Flutter

It's the Flutterball Final, and the
Naughty Fairies make an awesome
team, But their butterflies go missing
– and without them, there's no way
they can win. Can the Naughty
Fairies find the thieves and get their
butterflies back?

Ping's Wings

It's Bluebell Ball time, but the
Naughty Fairies have more to worry
about than their dresses. Ambrosia
Academy fairy Glitter has challenged
Ping to the Bramble Run: dangerous,
forbidden – and bound to end in
disaster!

Also available from
Hodder Children's Books

Potion Commotion

Detention is NOT Kelpie's idea of fun
on her flutterday. A trip to the beach
should make up for it! But when
uninvited guests pay a visit, it looks
as if Kelpie's flutterday is going to be
one BIG disaster.